To Joan Best

The

Wedding

Dress

...and Other Short Stories

Fiona Ballard

Copyright © 2022 Fiona Ballard

The moral right of the author has been asserted. All rights reserved, including the right to reproduce this book or portions thereof in any form whatsoever. No part of this book may be reproduced or transmitted in any form or by any means, electronic or mechanical, including photocopying, recording or by any information storage or retrieval system, without prior written permission from Fiona Ballard except for brief quotations in reviews. Nor be otherwise circulated in any type of binding or cover other than that in which it is published and without a similar condition including this condition being required of the purchaser.

THE WEDDING DRESS

Rouen

Henry the Eighth once said, 'Kent was the Garden of England,' but in recent times it had become more renowned for its houses, hop farms and apple orchards. Sabine Charbonneau was at home in Rouen, sitting in a familiar bedroom window seat, staring at a black and white wedding photograph. Reflecting on past events, she disagreed with the Tudor King's statement and found it difficult to correlate with the way her own life had unfolded. For a brief moment, her eyes focused one last time on the wedding album in her hand. Last time she had sat in the window seat she was wearing her wedding dress, made from parachute silk and designed by her mother. Intricately decorated with hand-sewn beads and tiny pearls that reflected the light in an exquisite shade of the palest pink. Without wishing to incur her father's wrath any further she ceased her daydreaming, shoved the photograph back in her overall pocket and returned to resume her bar cleaning duties.

Raoul Charbonneau, Sabine's father, was born in the town of Rouen, Normandy. The same town where Joan of Arc had lost her life, burnt at the stake on heresy charges. The town had changed little since those times in terms of its structure and appearance. It still bore quaint cobbled streets and gothic-looking gabled rooftops, painted in black or brown. Some of the buildings lent outwards towards the cobbles below, making them appear top-heavy. Each property offered structural support for the other, so they wouldn't topple forward to the street below. Being in a terrace of eight or so, the family bar La Belle Vie was positioned on the ground floor below.

The family surname Charbonneau came from a diminutive form of charbon or charcoal. Often used as a nickname for a person with raven hair just like Sabine. She chose to wear it in the traditional manner plaited and coiled in a circle on the back of her head. Azurine, her mother, was a seamstress for the rich and famous. She had a fine reputation not just in Rouen, but across the border into Brittany to the East and Picardie in the

North. The more opulent, affluent ladies of the region walked through her door to have their posh frocks and silk gowns altered in Azurine's parlour.

Raoul had descended from generations of veritable Normandy lineage. He had never been too bothered by his appearance, seldom approaching a mirror. With a mass of thick unkempt hair he shrugged off any interventions by Azurine to curtail his locks or shave his whiskers. To avoid her persistent scrutiny he'd hide his mop of hair under his prized possession, a scruffy black corduroy cap. One of his other quirks was wearing odd socks, as he disliked the chore of finding a pair that matched. Together the couple ran the local bar "La Belle Vie". Raoul was known locally as a font of all local knowledge. But that was a thin cover story for anything bought or sold under the counter of his bar. Counterfeit goods were still in circulation post-war. They were received and sold on with no questions asked, and a simple shrug of the shoulders. Raoul had a reputation across the region, nothing was written in ink and nothing discussed in detail or explained.

Their only daughter Sabine had been taught how to thread a needle and stitch the simplest of garments at a young age. Her mother had taught her how to sew delicate buttons and pearls onto yards of voluminous fabrics. Sabine was named after her Mother's elder sister, whose family had all been connected to the drapery and tailoring industry. Azurine had been blessed with a softer, less swarthy complexion than her daughter. Her eyes, a brilliant blue with pale lashes that sat in perfect proportions across her beatific face. The bright eyes of an optimist. Her own mane of auburn tresses ran in waves across the length of her back.

Recently she had been forced to wear spectacles with thin wiry frames to assist with the finer details of her dress making, acknowledging that age and sewing had taken its toll on her eyesight. Sabine recalled as a child how much she enjoyed watching her mother working late into the night, finishing a ballgown or a wedding dress. The dim golden light was always flickering in the corner of the family parlour, where the stove was at its warmest. The sewing machine would gently whirr away until the early hours as the deadlines for dresses came and went. The wooden pedal of the sewing machine clunked up and down in a rhythmic fashion beneath the table, worn into the shape of a small foot. The constant low drumming noise could be heard through the thin floorboards in the bedroom above where Sabine lay sleeping. She too had inherited a keen interest in fabrics, and as a teenager liked to experiment and make her own clothes. Sometimes she would scoop up the leftover fabrics from her mother's labours and squirrel them away in her bedroom for later use. The material from the fabric market would be different, either burgundy, brown or black and perhaps a heavier cord for the longer winter skirts. She only possessed one pair of blackened walking boots and these would come to serve her well in the coming months. Despite the coy looks under that dark curly mane she had a spark about her that appealed to the young men.

Claude and Jacques Deveraux, the twins fitted perfectly into her close-knit group. Her parents were oblivious to her comings and goings, or so she thought.

Wrapped up in their business, serving thirsty customers, she found it easy to fool them into thinking she was at a friend's house, when she was out meeting the twins.

It was during Sabine's morning shift, whilst cleaning the floor in the bar that Raoul decided to drop his bombshell.

"Sabine ma petite, sit down I've something to tell you," patting the seat, avoiding eye contact which she found strange. She preferred to stand anyway.

"I have volunteered for you to go to England and help with the harvest of apples and hops in Kent. It's part of a labour exchange programme. It means in return we will have some help in the bar". Whilst speaking he continued washing the dirty beer glasses and ashtrays in the sink. His thick-rimmed spectacles perched on the end of his nose not looking up, because if he'd raised his chin an inch he would have seen the expression of abject horror on his daughter's face. Sabine had been daydreaming leaving wet soapy streaks over the red linoleum floor, placing the mop back in the bucket. She stopped dead in her tracks, holding onto the mop to steady herself, she shook her head. Surely she had misheard him?

"Répétez vous Papa?" He preferred her to speak French, so he repeated his last sentence. There was to be no arguing with him he explained, she understood it was already a 'fait accompli'. The travel dates had been confirmed with the exchange agency.

"Tu rigoles oui?" "You are joking?"

"Non, non, Papa, J'ai mes propres plans pour l'été".

"I have my own plans for the summer," she wailed.

Her world had suddenly shattered into a thousand pieces. Raoul was ignorant of Sabine's plans made with the twins for the summer holidays. Tears welled as she propped the mop against the wall alongside the bucket and fled from the bar to the sanctuary of her bedroom. Leaving her father perplexed. Collapsing on the bed, sobbing into her damask pillow. Her father had now wrecked her plans, she hated him, he'd ruined her life!

Claude Deveraux had grown up on the outskirts of town on a dairy farm. Born under a Gemini star sign, figuratively speaking conjoined at the hip to his twin brother, Jacques. Claude's parents, Bernard and Fabienne owned a dairy farm and made their living from selling the milk and its by-products. They turned the rich, creamy liquid into butter, cheese or yoghurt. Growing up Claude, the elder twin by fifteen minutes, had been far more assertive, and self-assured than Jacques. Although he had a bad reputation for breaking hearts at senior school, he often had to rescue Jacques from scrapes at school. As non-identical twins, Jacques had blue eyes and his brother pale green but they both had the same texture of hair. Claude was born with few listening skills and a short fuse, a lethal combination in his brother's opinion. He seemed more concerned about his looks in the bathroom mirror than was entirely normal for a young man who grew up on a farm knee-deep in horse manure. In contrast Jacques the more thoughtful of the two, always held a deeper affection for their mother and matters of the heart. As youngsters, the twins did everything together despite their opposing personalities. The boys assisted their father Bernard, milking the dairy herd and making the cheese and yoghurt for distribution. The family had planned for the twins to inherit the farm estate, once they turned twenty-one. Or that's what they had always been led to believe!

Claude remembered the unreciprocated crush he had on Sabine Charbonneau back in the classroom. In those days he was a shy, gawky teenager, with glasses and greasy blonde curly hair. Claude knew he was not the hottest-looking teenager in the town. That ticket went to Guy Moreau who played in the school football team. Whenever Claude was in the presence of young women he would become awkward, tongue-tied and feel a blush creeping around his neck. If the girls struck up a conversation with him first, he wished to curl up in a ball with embarrassment. Thankfully those days were now far behind him. After his father's change of heart about the future of the farm. Their uncle stood to inherit the entire farm estate and not the twins. Bernard had quoted something about a new codicil to his will, after a sudden change of heart. Bitterly disappointed Claude decided to walk away from farming and take a different career path bidding farewell to the farm, he moved to Rennes to train as a Chef-cuisinier. When he returned from the training course he took a small first floor flat within a stone's throw of La Belle Vie.

Claude had been out on his rounds delivering some boxes of cheese to the weekly market. On impulse, he decided to stop off at the bar for a quick coffee. Whilst sipping his espresso he bumped into an old school friend, Sabine Charbonneau. It was the first time they had set eyes upon each other since leaving school.

The location seemed perfectly positioned for an eatery, just behind two Cathedrals in the central plaza. An archetypal Normandy Bistro with prettily painted royal blue shutters, and yellow gingham tablecloths covering square tables. Bottles of water and heavy coloured glasses stood in the centre, with serviettes tucked under the plates. The restaurant offered a varied

Plat du Jour which Claude took immense pride in delivering for his regular customers for a meagre three francs. Moule a La Creme, Agneau de Pre Sale or Salt Meadow Lamb, followed by Livarot cheese and to finish off a Normandy Apple Tart. Cheese would always be served before dessert in France, unlike England. For Sabine and Claude the reconnection of their friendship had happened by chance, born out of their love of French cuisine. If you peered out the loft window at the top of Sabine's house you could just see the outhouse at the far end of Claude's shared garden. It would soon become the place where they would meet in secret. But why was it necessary to meet in secret?

The two families had fallen out over a long-standing bitter feud, each siting their differences enough to deny the three youngsters a decent friendship. Neither father would consider a marital union of the two families, each one as stubborn and mule-headed as the other. Whenever the two men had the misfortune to meet in the street Bernard would cross over to the other side and grumble under his breath something about the

Charbonneau's being traitors. Such was the depth of their feelings, neither could remember how or why it had started. Both men believed they were right, a stance that had gone unresolved for many decades.

The new adult Claude was much better looking, with whorls of blonde curly hair, no longer greasy. The pale green eyes with petit features were unusual. Fabienne, his mother, had been so disappointed when the twins were born to discover that both babies were boys. As a baby Claude was often mistaken for a little girl, Fabienne indulged her fantasy and adorned him with frilly dresses.

But Sabine found it was Jacques who hovered in the background when she had been feeling smitten again, but which twin did she prefer? Until recently she could never really decide which one, the rambunctious one or the gentler more sensitive one. She had such little experience of men and so held nothing on which to base her sudden rush of feelings.

So Claude, Jacques and Sabine chose to keep their three-way friendship a secret. They smuggled samples of their cooking into the small outhouse, eager to impress each other with their culinary skills. It was here the three of them would share the delights of local homemade Couronne bread, or Tartes au Pomme. Sometimes it would be the cheese from the farm or some nicely aged Livarot, if available. Jacques kindly supplied the cheeses. Of course, Sabine had to smuggle the chocolate from under the counter in the bar.

Leaving the shyness and awkwardness of their teenage years behind them now as young adults their life couldn't have been more different. Their relationship that began six months ago had developed and now sex was no longer off-limits. Sabine found she liked to experiment and on a couple of occasions after a few glasses of Calvados, she had involved Jacques too. Their lives became inextricably entangled with Sabine who offered her services to both men, but in complete secrecy.

Sabine thought her cleaning chores were completed for the day, but when she checked her list it had suddenly become longer. Her father had asserted his authority again. This left her little time over the weekend to escape to the outhouse. He had become far too possessive of her time and looking back she wondered if this was a deliberate ploy to detain his only daughter under his watchful eye. So why did he sign her up for an exchange if he wanted to keep her at home under his authority? He refused to let her mature, and she wondered if he knew about her relationship with the twins? She hoped not, or at least the small intimate details. Since their earlier conversation in the bar, Sabine seemed more determined than ever to sabotage her father's plan for her to work in England. She had made up her mind, she would tell him she was not going and that was that. But was she strong enough to stand up to him.

Sabine Departs

The following day dawned with angry skies looking a threatening shade of purple, there was a storm brewing and not only in the skies. The rains returned in torrential, slanting sheets. Sabine had not had a spare minute to tell Claude the news about her impending trip, her father had kept her so busy. It was her own fault she had left it until the last minute. By breakfast time the storm was in full swing. Looking out across the rooftops she noticed the window of the outhouse was open, despite the rain. This was Claude's secret sign that he was waiting for her, often in anticipation. Determined to see him before leaving for England she set aside her cleaning trug, and exited the back door. Braving the rain bouncing off the path, Sabine took her chance pulling her favourite black shawl over her head. Running the short distance to the outhouse her frock quickly became saturated. How would she break the news to Claude? This was not going to be an easy conversation and she felt the tension rise in her throat, as the door opened.

"I have something to tell you Claude," she blurted without so much as a 'hello 'or a welcome kiss. She took off her sodden shawl and shook her hair spraying the drops of rain everywhere like a dog shaking it's coat. Claude kissed her cheek and at that moment he realised that he loved her far more than she loved him. Shrugging him off she started to explain but her words tumbled out in the wrong order. Didn't he see that this would ruin all their plans? Claude stood back and studied her face, trying to make sense of the words.

"Calm down Sabine, what are you talking about?"

"My father has arranged for me to go to England tomorrow on a labour exchange. That's what I have been trying to tell you," Claude tried his best to interrupt,

"It is against my wishes, but I have no choice. What can I do?" her voice cracking.

"Now he has ruined our plans, I hate him, I hate him," sobbing into his shoulder.

"Why don't we leave now, run away to Picardie, then we can still marry as we planned?". It sounded like the typical plan of somebody who failed to think through the consequences. She had told no one about her affair with the brothers. Many households have their dark secrets bubbling just below the surface, and the Charbonneau family was no different. Claude's suggestion of an elopement had crossed her mind but she knew it would break her mother's heart if she left without saying goodbye. And Picardie why choose there, she knew nobody? Had he considered Jacques? Claude had proposed to Sabine some months ago, but she had declined. Not wishing to incur her father's wrath. After a minute he locked the door and they forgot everything for a few brief moments as Claude initiated sex on the sofa. It happened in an urgent clinging sort of way, both knowing it would be the last time for a while. Keen to get on with it now he had her to himself, Claude sighed heavily leaving Sabine breathless and still bewildered.

The following day she would be heading for England, leaving those she loved behind, unsure when she would return again. She felt obliged to take Azurine & Jacques into her confidence at the last minute, they were the only ones privy to their secret plan. But Jacques and Claude would play a key part in the escape plan from England back to Rouen. Insistent that Raoul should be kept in the dark, as he would be too tempted to scupper their plans. But how would Azurine feel about keeping a secret from her husband? Sabine was not convinced that her mother wouldn't crumble under pressure.

The Dress

As fabric and francs were still in short supply in terms of creating a wedding dress, a degree of thriftiness would be required by Azurine. Sabine asked where she would acquire the lace and silk to make the dress. Azurine already knew the answer. The women discussed at length the shape, style and fabric that Sabine wanted for her wedding day.

Jacques offered to acquire the main part of the wedding dress which would be cream silk through his contacts. He explained that he knew of a parachute factory alongside the river, where boats unloaded mysterious crates, late at night. Confident that under the cover of darkness, a theft could take place without drawing too much attention. The parachutes were only slightly damaged, then discarded in large container bins at the rear of the factory; considered not fit for reuse. Timing was all important and a boat with a quiet engine. The moon would need to be at its thinnest and the night sky at its darkest.

Jacques would drop off the parachute to Azurine who was more than happy to make a start on cutting out the shape of the dress. By the end of that day Sabine felt a little happier that her escape plan was coming together and she met with Jacques in the outhouse to express her thanks in her usual way. Jacques had not yet expressed his true feelings either. How would she choose between the two brothers?

Although the dress pattern was familiar, Azurine still had to double check there were enough jewels to decorate the front panel. Her only reservation would be trying to fit the bodice without the presence of the bride. But Azurine would not let that faze her. She had decided to make it a size larger in case Sabine gained weight whilst working on the farm.

She hoped her daughter was not planning anything crazy with Claude as Sabine remained blissfully unaware that her parents knew about their relationship. Raoul had spotted her returning through the garden, late at night when he was locking up the bar. And then Azurine had gone upstairs to ask her a question about her trip to England and found her bed empty. She chose not to say anything to her husband for fear of inflaming an already delicate situation. Raoul, knowing his beloved daughter would soon be gone, said nothing as he too was having second thoughts about what he had done. How would she handle the language barrier, would her limited English be sufficient? It was too late to abort the trip. He would lose face among his contacts.

The Penance

Sabine knew her penance would be fully served by the end of the exchange trip. But she had no intention of staying the full three months and would pull out of the arrangement early. Everything had been taken care of by her father, nothing left to chance. Clutching her first passport in a trembling hand she said her goodbyes, hugging her parents, before walking to the station. The wooden train chugged its way out of town and the protracted journey to Dunkerque. Fortunately for Sabine it had pulled out of the station before she could change her mind. Sitting in a cramped carriage she chose to stare out of the window in an attempt to distract herself. The other passengers had taken an interest in this young woman with her brown holdall bag and a small basket. A solitary tear appeared on her cheek as she blinked, she tried putting Claude and Jacques to the back of her mind.

The gruesome journey took nearly two days. The worst part was the lumpy sea with white froth that made her stomach lurch. She was met at the Dunkerque ferry terminal by a farm hand who collected up the new recruits. The final leg of her journey found her perched high on a torn leather seat of a rickety farm truck. The main road out of the port took them on a circuitous route along the main Folkstone Road to the village of Alkham. Here they were welcomed by a farm manager called Frank, and the overpowering sweet scent of ripened apples. At first it was all too much to take in. The farm vehicles emitted a strong smell of burning diesel to add to the heady atmosphere of over ripened fruits.

Before leaving, Raoul had promised that her job would be only picking the local apple & hop harvest, but his words strayed far from the truth as the job was far more punishing. On her first morning Sabine, like the other starters, was allocated to the fruit picking team. After twelve hour shifts she fell into bed exhausted, the pungent musty smell from her bedding lingering in her nostrils. The small metal bed rattled whenever she turned over and had a mattress that made her itch and scratch. She believed she had not been the only thing sharing the bed! Last thing at night before going to sleep, a cameo of her mother would come into her mind. Azurine would be sitting in her favourite chair in the parlour at home, creating miracles with many coloured threads, beads and bobbins, surrounded by reams of fabric. Was Sabine hiding something else? Had she grown too close to Claude, or maybe Jacques? Azurine's maternal assumptions about her daughter had been correct and made a wise decision to add an inch or two to the wedding dress. Towards the end of the second month Sabine carefully organised her escape with the help of Claude and Jacques. Letters had been coming to and fro to confirm their latest plan and the last envelope contained her return ferry ticket. Sabine would escape on the nightly apple truck run to the port. The brothers would come to Dunkerque, and drive her back to Rouen where they planned to marry? What could possibly go wrong? Would she make it back in time to marry her childhood sweetheart and the love of her life? But, had Sabine been truly faithful to Claude? Somebody would need to book the local Notaire to officiate La Marriage on her return. The last letter had also stated that all the preparations were in hand and she was not to worry. That was typical of Claude, a kind message to reassure her and calm her anxieties.

Not long after her arrival Sabine had worked out what was causing her loss of appetite. She still helped herself to any food offered, and hid it away until her morning nausea subsided, later in the day. Sometimes she was able to nibble on a piece of stale bread at night, her body simply craving nourishment and the stomach growls indicating her hunger had gone unrewarded. It was a secret she had kept to herself during the last couple of weeks: the feeling of nausea combined with extreme tiredness and fatigue. Was it her imagination or was her waistline thickening slightly too? Her breasts had become tender when she put on her liberty bodice. The pickers had no mirrors in their rooms so she was unable to check for changes to her belly. Her chief concern had been the wedding dress; it may not fit, despite Azurine taking accurate measurements before she left.

"You're daydreaming again," barked Frank the farm manager for the umpteenth time that day.

"Get on with your job young lady, there are more apples to pick and trucks to be loaded!" Sabine gave him a hard mono brow stare. She clearly annoyed him. Had she made it that obvious? So why did he shout at her so often? She believed it was because she was French. Frank was quite right she was daydreaming, she was also striking off the days left with her peeling knife. Cursing her father as she gouged out the strikes on a tree. Her hands were red raw and itchy, the skin split between her fingers, despite wearing her new finger gloves. Her knees pockmarked with grazes from the kneeling on the stones that surrounded the trees and bushes.

The outside temperature was rising by the day, summer had finally arrived. The workers rose at five and started work at six working through until sundown. They were lucky if they got to sit down on a straw bale for ten minutes a day, the farm conditions had a reputation for being harsh. They were served cheese and bread for lunch, handed out from the dirty apple crates. You either ate what was offered or went hungry.

There had been urgent things on Sabine's mind, after the hops had been picked, each row of apple trees in the orchard had to be stripped of its fruit. Often the weight of the apples in the bags strapped around their waists became too heavy to handle. Every crate had to be stacked ten high to enable the truck to take them into the pressing area. The movement of raising her arms above her head occasionally made her feel a little lightheaded, forcing her to sit down just out of Frank's sight.

Sabine learnt quickly that the pressing area had been feared by labourers the most. It was full of lethargic wasps that waited till your head turned away before zooming in and landing on your arm or worse in your ear. Or if you were really unlucky they would land on your neck out of sight, firing their venom under your skin. The pickers were advised to carry a small amount of vinegar on a cloth in your pocket, to remove the itchy sting.

There had been plenty of other jobs around the farm that the girls were expected to share. Once the apple press had been loaded with it's golden treasures and the amber nectar released, the farm workers could ease off their duties a little and take a break. At the end of the day the shout would come from down the line, starting with Frank at the far end.

"Pick no more bines," came the signal, meaning to down tools. Other workers would set upon you immediately if you failed to stop when the call went up.

Sabine found out to her cost and learnt fast. One girl had walloped her on the back with a basket for not stopping when told. At the time she was more shocked by her reaction and swore at her in French. Was this why she had not been so easily persuaded to make friends with the other farm workers? There was a natural language barrier and the jokes in English had not translated so well into French, the irony wasted. Sabine decided there was no point in building friendships as she was planning to remove herself as soon as possible.

She had been keeping one little secret from her employers, and communications between the farm and home in the form of written letters from Rouen had dwindled. She believed that Frank had deliberately misplaced the incoming letters as he had taken such a dislike to her. But the final letter that arrived was from Jacques not Claude, declaring his love for Sabine. What should she do knowing that she was now the object of both men's affections?

The growing bump would soon need a father and Sabine had to choose, but she liked them both. Who was the baby's father? Had she been unfaithful to Claude?

The notches on the apple tree told her that the days at the farm had come to an end. She double counted them just to ensure her calculations had been correct. Yes, the time had come to leave. She was unable to last the full term of her contract due to the physical limitations on her body. Frank was about to discover her secret. Her escape from purgatory had to be that night.

The Escape

Everything was arranged, Sabine would escape the fruit farm that night, once darkness had descended. The night sky was perfect, silky black with no clouds. A couple of howling foxes, but otherwise quiet. Leaving the sleeping huts, her bag slung over her shoulder, she walked carefully along the track trying to avoid any pot holes. In a clearing stood a line of waiting lorries. They left at regular intervals taking the apples to sell in France. She had practised the route many times in her head but in the darkness of reality it all seemed different. A crackling in the trees to the left, had this meant her cover was blown? Phew, only a fox or badger? At the first lorry, she wriggled her body under the heavy khaki tarpaulin, tearing her shawl on the side of the truck. Slithering into place whilst trying not to breathe, she could hear a familiar thumping in her ribcage. Disoriented by strange noises outside the truck, Sabine held her breath again until it all went quiet. Two deep Kentish accents approached the truck, opening and slamming the cab doors. The damp engine coughed and spluttered, turned over two or three times before chugging into life. The wagon started to vibrate, as it headed out to the main road towards Dover. Sabine thought she was going to be sick as the truck flung her body from side to side, she wished she hadn't eaten supper. Could she vomit quietly? she was unsure. She attempted to wedge herself firmly between the crates to get more comfortable. How many more roundabouts were there going to be making the truck lurch like that? She tried to swallow hard and keep herself from retching.

The grand master plan had been to transfer from the truck to the ferry then disembark with the ferry passengers through the terminal, to the Roulier du Port Ouest exit, where her escorts would be waiting.

The Reunion

Sabine had been looking forward to her reunion with Claude and Jacques, and this single thought had kept her going through some very dark days back on the farm. For the moment she put them to the back of her mind as she needed to focus. The customs inspection honed in on every other lorry and her luck held. First she wriggled out from under the tarpaulin. She waited till the ferry was about to set sail and made her way with the other foot passengers out to the upper decks, clutching her ferry ticket just in case.

To her astonishment it was quite easy to mingle amongst the ferry crowds. An hour later they docked and Sabine made herself inconspicuous among the queue of people waiting to disembark.

The rendezvous area was through the terminal building, as she drew closer she panicked as she couldn't see either Claude or Jacques. Checking and rechecking the signage to ensure she was at the correct exit, yes she was in the right place. She looked at her watch again. The date and time were correct. Perhaps the traffic was heavy and they had been held up? Or they had started out late? Maybe a puncture? Or worse, had an accident? She had speculated. Each permutation ran wild through her mind and she began to perspire under her arms with the stress and anxiety of the moment.

The Accident

On the far side of the terminal perimeter fence, Sabine heard the sound of emergency sirens wailing, turning her head, she walked towards the source. On the right-hand side of the road she spotted a blue Citroen police car alongside a red and white ambulance with its doors flung wide open and a commotion inside, the voices were raised. The emergency workers had been carrying a stretcher with a static body, covered by a white sheet. It looked like there had been a fatality, she shivered as she approached the police barrier. Behind the vehicles at the roundabout she spotted a familiar car, it seemed to be a very peculiar shape squashed at right angles into a second car. Yes, that was Claude's vehicle. The flesh of the two pieces of metal seemed to blend into one another.

The road remained closed. The police were directing the traffic using hand signals, with long outstretched arms attached to their large white gloves. As Sabine approached, she noticed the man sitting on the brick wall was her beloved Jacques, who looked up just at that moment. He struggled to stand as they fell into each other's arms hugging gently, unable to let go. But where was Claude?

"Oh no," she whispered, grasping her mouth. Just one look at Jacque's face said enough. Her face turned ashen and her legs wobbled, she was going to faint just as the sky faded from her peripheral vision. Sabine dropped slowly to her knees onto the pavement. Yes she had fainted.

When she came to, she found herself lying on a coat shaking uncontrollably, hugging her body and the small bump under her sweater. The medics explained they had tried their best, but were unable to save Claude. When Jacques finally composed himself he felt able to relay the rest of the story.

The journey from Rouen had started late, and they had been in a rush to meet her, when the car suddenly burst a front tyre. Claude struggled to steer, spinning out of control as it smashed headlong into the oncoming car. The poor man stood no chance taking the full impact of the two vehicles moving at speed. This was not supposed to happen, not part of their escape plan! The police officer held up his hand and bellowed again cursing at the traffic.

They had to formally identify Claude, and Jacques was registered as the next of kin at the hospital. Sabine noted the mortuary was alongside the oncology wards and shook her head in disbelief. Why would you design a building as such? When the pair were finally released by the police and the hospital they set off to find the railway station, for a silent journey back to Rouen. Who would be the one to tell the families? How would they get Claude's body back to Rouen? The funeral directors based at the hospital had offered to collect the body from the morgue and deliver the coffin back to Rouen. But this subject had been totally overshadowed by events of the last few hours. Sabine did not wish to think about the wedding and her expanding waistline as she was grieving for poor Claude.

The pair arrived back a little after midnight having talked through the various options on the journey. They walked through the deserted streets arriving at La Belle Vie bar. Pausing by the back door to hug and say goodbye, they spotted Sabine's father sitting alone at the bar. Supping his nightcap, a shot of Calvados, and smoking his last Gitane of the day. Catching sight of the pair he rushed out of the door with many questions.

"Where was Claude, and why were Sabine and Jacques holding hands and kissing?".

"You are shivering mon petit, come inside you are so cold," said her father. He poured two more glasses of Calvados and set them on the bar. Azurine, hearing a commotion came rushing downstairs, in her robe and mules. As they broke the news about Claude she embraced the youngsters, and tried hard to maintain her composure. They were both overjoyed to see their daughter safely home. Was it Azurine's imagination but did she look a little fuller round the waistline? Her maternal assumption had been correct. Jacques finished his drink and returned to the farm to let his parents know about Claude. Jacques didn't know how he was going to break it to her, his mother would be bereft.

The Funeral

The Notaire had been notified by Jacque's parents that there had been a death in the family. At his pre-funeral visit he presented them with a list of things to do, and one in particular was most important. He would only attend the funeral with the body inside the coffin. These were the rules of his church. Adding of course that it was at the family's discretion whether the lid was open or shut, he didn't mind that part. He recalled that he had recently attended a funeral where the body was not placed in a coffin and he was unable to commit it for burial.

Another family tradition that had been in Sabine's family for generations concerned the use of honey. They believed that honey connected the souls of the deceased so by leaving the jars of liquid nectar open around the body to attract the flies, meant they held the souls of the deceased.

As they gathered at the farmhouse awaiting the hearse, Bernard had taken a walk alone in the garden to gather his thoughts. He asked to speak with Jacques and

Sabine alone before the end of the day. Jacques had offered to read the eulogy about growing up with a twin on behalf of his parents. He thought a few school friends would appreciate his injection of humour. Sabine had chosen the flowers, white lilies, Claude's favourite.

At least the sun was shining even though the crows sitting in the treetops at the farm entrance were announcing to the neighbourhood that the mortals had lost another soul. The funeral car gathered Bernard and Fabienne and delivered them a short distance to the small chapel. Jacques had chosen to travel separately in the family Citroen, to be alone for a moment with Sabine. The coffin was gently lowered onto the trolley by the pallbearers and guided through the chapel. As the doors opened the two large white candles flickered on the altar table making the folded edges of the cloth sway. The organist started to play, and the congregation stood up. Jacques read the eulogy and a couple of friends emitted a few false laughs, as they remembered Claude. He managed to reach the end before he was overcome by the occasion. Afterwards Rouel and Azurine had organised a small family wake in the bar at their own expense. For a brief moment the families had forgotten the feud.

The Wedding

A few weeks later when everything had settled down and the funeral formalities were completed, discussions at La Belle Vie turned to the wedding. Sabine had made up her mind, it would go ahead despite the tragic demise of Claude. She had explained to her parents that she would now be marrying Jacques. What had brought about this change of heart her father asked? At this point she should have told him about the baby's father, but chose to keep it a secret for a bit longer. She asked only two things of him; that the family dispute be put to one side, and to promise her he would be ready to leave for the church at 11 a.m. to give her away. If they delayed or postponed any further Sabine would no longer fit into her wedding dress. It was already feeling snug. The wedding guest list was shortened to immediate family only. Pierre, a friend of Jacques's, who worked as a newspaper photographer at the Liberte Dimanche had kindly stepped in to take the wedding photographs.

The bride looked radiant on the day, as she waited for her father in the bar, holding a small posy of lilac and pink flowers to match the floral headband. Azurine stood back to admire her work, she felt relieved, the wedding dress was a neat fit. The local Notaire, Monsieur Marais officiated the ceremony and in the circumstances agreed to waive his fee. Both sets of parents unaware that the grandchild Sabine was carrying was not Claude's, but Jacques. Another conversation for another day, thought Sabine.

"Sourire, smile, regarde le camera, look straight at the camera," said Pierre, as she clutched her bouquet to hide the now expansive bump. The camera flashed and everybody squinted into the early afternoon sunshine.

"Next... deux set de parents s'il vous plait, the two sets of parents please," Jacques was having difficulty manoeuvring people into their rightful places. The groom had scrubbed up well and was wearing his brother's brown tweed suit, and brown polished brogues. The mothers shed a few happy tears into their hankies, and the fathers managed to secure a firm handshake, forgetting their differences for just a day.

Petit Michel

A few months later, with the cruel memories of the farm in Kent now fading, Sabine was sitting in her bedroom at her dressing table staring at the mirror. She let out a long sigh and carefully returned the crumpled wedding photograph to the tiny wooden box alongside the one of her baby son. She held him close to her, inhaling that special baby scent at the nape of his neck. Placing Petit Michel alongside her in his wooden crib, his smooth tanned legs started to kick. For now the happier wedding memories had been firmly recorded by Pierre and arranged in a beautiful album as a wedding present. In another change of heart, and a subtle nod to Claude, Jacques had been left the farm by his father. Sabine would become a farmer's wife and take over the production of the dairy products. Jacques had become an attentive husband and a devoted father to Michel, who had been born out of love. When the baby smiled his toothless gummy smile, he reminded Sabine of his uncle Claude, and she knew she had made the right decision.

THE CHOCOLATE BOX REUNION

In the precinct, the chocolate shop known locally as 'Melting Moments 'had been the only place in town where you could buy authentic chocolates. The sumptuous window displays lured many a passer by with a weak willed nature, into their chocolate kingdom. The Chocolate Tasting Club met once a month to critique the latest tastes and flavours on the market, culminating usually with a vote at the end of the evening. But this had been a special occasion, a celebratory birthday dinner where the attendees had all been dark chocolate connoisseurs. The chocolates had been designed to impress and tempt the audience that evening with the twelve dark chocolate flavours and sizes. The luxurious fillings had been lovingly decorated and laid out carefully in a hexagonal pattern. The box had been exquisitely packaged and tied up with a large red bow then set at a clever jaunty angle amongst the opulent window display. Always aimed at eye level to catch the browsing customer's eye, the chosen box had been given a luxurious lining of soft burgundy velvet with golden star sprinkles scattered among the folds of the fabric.

Inside the box, hidden amongst that smooth burgundy velvet had been twelve mischievous chocolates all with their individual personalities. When left to their own devices they were ready to spring to life, within the strictest of pecking orders already firmly established amongst the group of chocolate co-habitants. To understand the story of Tangerine Dreamer and her chocolate friends the introductions should start with her at centre stage. She was the only chocolate with a wrapper of gold foil with a plush silver lining, the highest honour. In such a prestigious position within the box and always top of the rankings in terms of popularity. Tangerine Dreamer was of course shaped like a slice of tangerine with a scent that would usually only be associated with cloves, cinnamon and Christmas celebrations. Not at all like the ball shaped Chocolate Oranges clogged together in a square box.

Tangerine Dreamer had a smooth pale orange filling covered in a rich silky dark chocolate. Always giving out the orders and rearranging the box to suit herself, she liked to be centre stage, but also considered herself as 'Director of Operations'.

Carmel Fudge, the most popular choice with the younger ones, had always been made so soft and sticky in the centre. More often to be seen and sold in small stripy paper bags at the funfair. Carmel Fudge disliked being placed too close to the others as any heat had always affected her insides. The fruitier flavoured ones had always stuck together in a clustered group for they had often heard that there had been more security and less temptation in numbers.

Choc-A-Block had been such a different personality from all the others, holding the honour of being the only male in the selection box, as he held no flavour in his centre. A solid piece of dark chocolate to sink your teeth into but, once on the tongue simply melted you away with pure ecstasy. A macho rather toughened character. Completing daily workouts to keep his prime image up to date with a perfected ripped effect, that was vitally important to him. Popular with the rest of the team as they could use him to clamber up to other sections of the box. This however was not really allowed according to Carmel Fudge the Health and Safety Coordinator. One or two of the other chocolates never listened. Choc-A-Block always liked to assist the females in the boxes where possible.

Honeycomb Heather had a brain full of fizzing golden coloured air bubbles, making her just a little bit light headed and more often than not a little bit ditsy. But that could have just been the over-excitement and the upheaval of their later move. Recently she had thoroughly enjoyed having all her old familiar friends around her to catch up with the latest gossip about who was in and out of flavour amongst the team.

Turkish Rosewater was a bit of a late starter and unsure what to think about her own popularity. Some of the other chocolates hadn't taken kindly to the strong overpowering scent, especially when the lid went down on the box, filling their airspace with a lingering, cloying odour. Certainly the most fragrant of all the chocolates, with a deep rose pink jelly encased in a rippled dark chocolate coating. She had great difficulty in making any firm friends, usually keeping herself to herself in the corner, protecting her jelly filling.

Coffee Bean Betty had a simple coffee bean placed very carefully on the top of her chocolate arrangement, mid-centre. Always the pacifier in the group, keen to calm things down when things got overheated and anxious situations took hold. This had normally happened when two or three chocolates were pre-selected for an early consumption, often put to one side out of sight without the chance to say any farewells.

Strawberry Surprise took her name from a popularity poll among the shop customers, due to the soft dark surprise when it first hit the mouth and the tongue. The centre just oozed a smooth pink velvety softness. Soft and creamy but very sweet despite the coating she was quite a chunky chocolate compared to the others.

Lime Cordial had a sparkly but slightly acidic flavour with a luminous green centre. Covered in silky chocolate, so tangy and fruity leaving a tingling on the taste buds. This chocolate shrugged off all the name calling (Limey) and settled in for the long haul. Lime Cordial would usually be the last one chosen. The last choice in the box as a result of being thrown away in the rubbish bin, she had grown a toughened exterior.

Ginger Delight always warmed the tongue with a subtle but gentle fiery heat, often thought to be too aromatic when sealed in a small confined space. The ginger had originated from the Sanskrit (meaning horned root) but there had been definitely no horns in this chocolate selection. The price of the box of chocolates from Melting Moments had always reflected the elevated costs, but the chocolates didn't care much for all the theorising.

Vanilla Vera had always boasted that her origins were even slightly more exotic than the others and originated in Madagascar to be precise. Often unpopular in taste but yet such an excellent flavour enhancer found in so many sweets, desserts or cakes, and always top of any baking recipe ingredients list. The others agreed she was a bit dreary.

Black Cherry Delight had a deeper dark side, a little fleshy in the middle and sumptuous to the taste. One of the first most popular choices straight out of the box with a bold flavoured fruit and a hard centre of stone. Quite bossy in nature because she thought she was always a cut above the rest of the chocolates. Preferring to remain in the same position in the box, so woe betide anyone for sliding into her shell space. She had only been willing to move along to another space as and when absolutely forced(usually by Choc a Block but always under protest!)

Coconut Icer had been the loose canon among them, frivolous by name and frivolous by nature. Coloured in the centre with pink and white stripes and fun loving with many lacy frills but really not intellectually or emotionally gifted compared to the others. She had developed a nervous giggling habit at all the antics of her chocolate friends.

Back at home the dining room normally used for special occasions, was the chosen location for the evening tasting session. Decorated and arranged in a smart Art Deco style, with deep red walls, displaying a large gold edged mirror hanging above the 1920's sleek sideboard.

The table and chairs had all been recently purchased to complete the style. The pretty conch shell lamps were a matching pair placed at either end of the mantelpiece, emitting a warm soft ambience around the room. The long oak sanded floorboards held a trapdoor in the corner under which lay hidden such a variety of chocolate wrappers from a long held secret. Gold, silver, red, blue, green, purple, they were all there. You required a strong torchlight to pick them out. The dining room had seen many tenants over the years, but never a box of chocolates which had held such significance. However, tonight had been such a special night which warranted the finest chocolates to be devoured and savoured by the Chocolate Club with the chief taster celebrating turning thirty.

Much to the horror of the chocolates the celebrations involved four large pink, lighted candles! For the chocolates their worst nightmare was heat. Cookers, candles, fireworks, sparklers, it really didn't matter. They were all seen as "No No's" and had to be avoided at all costs. Nobody wanted to be too close in case their outer coats melted into an ominous dark chocolate puddle.

After dinner, like a children's game of pass the parcel, the chocolate box commenced a full table circuit from warm hand to warm hand. The box passed painfully slowly round the table, tilted one way and then the other. With the visitor's stomachs now satiated, stuffed full of Beef Bourguignon and Key Lime Pie, there had been little room or desire for any chocolate tasting. The red wine had flowed nicely amongst the visitors. But the guests, with their bellies so full were unable to move an inch, and needed much persuasion to taste any more chocolates. The vote for the tastiest chocolate was unanimous, Tangerine Dreamer. At this point the chocolates noticed two of them were missing. Ah what a shame, Coconut Icer hadn't made it! Wait a minute! There was another space, lovely Coffee Bean Betty had vanished too.

They only knew this as the coffee bean had been rudely discarded back in the box. This was really sad as she was always the one to tell them a night time story after lights out when the lid went back on. At last the box had ended up resting on the sideboard albeit in a slightly ruffled and dishevelled looking state.

Being midsummer the chocolates often went into meltdown mode behaviour, when the outdoor thermometer reached temperatures above 40 degrees. Anxiety levels had always been elevated until the rooms had cooled down towards the evening to a more bearable heat. But on this particular evening the heat hadn't diminished as promised by the weather app, it had increased. As a result the remaining chocolates had been swiftly packed up. The rumour in the box was that they were all heading down the passageway towards the kitchen and then 'Oh No 'their worst possible nightmare. Not the FRIDGE! Never recommended for luxury chocolate storage, far too cold for a start, they required an ambient temperature. Not wishing to panic the box but there had always been a strict hierarchy and jostling of position within the fridge. On a previous occasion this had not ended well, with all the chocolates suffering from hypothermia.

As part of the kitchen refurbishment a glossy full length fridge with chrome double doors with a fancy instant ice maker had been installed. The glistening worktop made of expensive pink granite had a slightly longer shelf life than their own chocolate box. The pecking order of the fridge community was sacrosanct and no one would argue that fact. The top shelf, reserved purely for the dairy products such as yoghurts, cream, butter and cheeses, some more powerful in aroma than others (especially the awful French stinkers!). All the same it had always been strictly dairy products only. The middle shelf stored some cooked chicken mango skewers, cold meats and a spicy chorizo sausage. In a blue ceramic dish there was some leftover Shepherds Pie from the day before, covered in plastic cling film. The chocolates detested cling film as it always gathered water droplets underneath it's surface and made their own contents soggy. The bottom shelf had held a nightmare for the chocolates, the worst possible location. A box containing a vegetarian pizza smothered in mozzarella cheese, basil and some fancy sun dried tomatoes. A large square box with greasy stains on the lid for such a small inconsequential pizza, according to the chocolates. Hanging out of the side was a used red serviette. At the bottom there had been a new vegetable box that kept all the vegetables and salads at a lower temperature. There would obviously be a strict pecking order within the fridge and if, as the chocolates suspected, it looked likely that they would be relegated to sharing a shelf with the oversized pizza box yuk, yuk, yuk.

"I'm not sharing a shelf with that pizza box," lamented poor Vanilla Vera. Their own box had been far superior in terms of colour, layering, fabric and quality.

"Why should we be squashed up in the corner?" whinged Turkish Rosewater.

"I'm not happy either," wailed Ginger Delight to no one in particular. She didn't really know why she had been protesting, she had just wanted to fit in with the others. It had been so hard to quell all their fears and frustrations with the latest accommodation changes.

Strawberry Surprise had been the first to comment that the temperature in the kitchen alone had been somewhat cooler than the dining room with all those dreadful spitting and sputtering pink candles. But it was too late for Carmel Fudge, who unfortunately had already got a slightly gooey problem of her own to deal with. Placed closest to the group of candles she had already suffered a bit of her own melt down. The fudge had started to ooze out of her middle in a long thin stripe. This meant nobody would want to eat her anyway.

"Hurrah I'm saved," she laughed!

Honeycomb Heather had already made a somewhat controversial comment about the sub zero temperatures in the fridge and how would they all manage without any wrappers to keep them warm? She reminded the chocolates about their inbox training they received last month, advising them how to avoid low temperatures as it had affected the composition of their outer chocolate coatings. Depending where you sat with this particular opinion it could be seen as a bad thing or even a good thing? Honeycomb Heather had struggled to convince the entire box, some had been more bolshy and sceptical about the training than others.

Time for the latest pep talk as the conversations had been getting heated. To avoid panic Choc a Block took charge.

"We must all stick together, in times of a crisis remember what we agreed?".

The tarnished glasses stained with a dark ruby red lipstick along with the chocolates had made it as far as the new snazzy kitchen worktop on a round metal tray. But now another chocolate was discovered missing. It had been the chocolate centrepiece, this was a disaster. Where was Tangerine Dreamer, her golden blanket wrapper was nowhere to be seen? No sign of it scrunched up or abandoned on the worktop. So there was no reason why Tangerine Dreamer couldn't make it back into the box with a lucky rabbit's foot and a fair wind or was it the other way round! Choc a Block couldn't remember which way round the saying went. It would need a happy miracle though, but it hadn't been beyond the realms of possibility, as he had tried his best to reassure them all. There was always the backup plan. They would need to keep alert to the sound of the lid of the box shuffling and scratching during the next few hours. Ginger Delight finally brought them all to their senses with some happy confectionery top hit songs such as 'Sweets for My Sweets 'or 'Sugar Sugar 'the most popular ones to start or 'Life on Mars Bars 'to follow!

The fridge had been cleaned in preparation. The glass shelves had been wiped down with a bright pink dish cloth and some rather potent cleanser. That smell lingered too long and certainly tarnished the food taste despite all its claims on the bottle. Well, it was certainly going to happen whether they approved of it or not. Before closing the fridge door the birthday girl picked up the chocolates and put them on the bottom shelf of the fridge. As she was shutting the door and turned round to go, oh no the chocolates saw the crescent moon shape outline of Tangerine Dreamer.

The birthday girl had put her in the back pocket of her navy skinny jeans for a sneaky chocolate binge, when all her overfed chocoholic guests had departed. Not the best place in the world because she would be squashed flat as a pancake by the time it came to eating her. The rather ample but rounded back side overfilled the jeans, spilling over into a muffin top. Having grown a little broader in the beam over the last year, she would have benefitted from a regular workout. Or perhaps an exercise bike routine? Tangerine Dreamer had stood little or no chance or had she? The chocolates hoped against hope she hadn't sat down on the way to the kitchen!

The shame of sharing a bottom fridge shelf with a Pizza Box, would they ever live it down, what an insult! But, how could they avoid this? Lime Cordial and Vanilla Vera who had always been the best of friends had a really clever idea. Conveniently, the box had been left wide open with the lid half off so they could tip themselves out and hide in a huddle elsewhere. The only problem they could think of was where should they go. The garden shed had been out of the question with too many obstacles and a long arduous journey, with many dangers on the way. Somewhere in the kitchen remained their safest bet, maybe at the back of a cool cupboard?

Once the kitchen sink duties had been duly completed, the dishwasher was safely loaded and the red start button set to go, beep , beep and it kicked into life. There was a brief interlude where the remaining chocolates were in deep discussion safely in their box just trying to hold it steady, as Choc A Block took control. The fridge had been left to dry out after a thorough cleansing routine with the door slightly ajar, what luck! This was their golden opportunity to escape. In charge of engineering and strategy was Black Cherry Surprise. Following the strictest of instructions, they went quietly about their business making a ramp out of the box lining, starting on the bottom shelf and ending up almost on the kitchen floor. Their luck was in, there had been a kitchen footstool left innocently by the door, if they were careful they could slither down it. Chatter had to be kept to a minimum as they helped one another master the rather bumpy homemade ramp, landing in a bit of a heap but with all outer coatings of chocolate still intact.

"Phew" they thought, "a very lucky escape indeed!" At this point they had really missed their two close chocolate box friends Coffee Bean Betty and Coconut Icer. But they had not mourned too much as the latest gossip on the chocolate grapevine had been about a certain chocolate connection between Strawberry Surprise and Choc A Block, as they had seemed to have become inseparable.

This had been a welcome distraction and something else to think about, although it was always understood that chocolates in a box, especially such the superior and delectable ones as themselves, would always be targets for gluttony.

Once on the kitchen floor they had followed their leader in the direction of the long blue cupboard set at an angle across the far corner of the kitchen. They found comfort and plenty of space to hide amongst the baking sheets and kitchen foil at the bottom of the really useful cupboard.

Just after midnight the lady of the house returned downstairs this time wrapped in her pink fluffy dressing gown and matching flip flop slippers. The switch for the copper overhead kitchen lights clicked. Stopping right in her tracks, she noted the fridge door was ajar. She didn't remember doing that. Had it been the result of too much red wine, how many bottles had been drunk? No matter though, the large box must have nudged it open. Removing the pizza box and tipping its remaining contents out onto a pink side plate, she prepared for a midnight feast. Stopping dead in her tracks she noticed the entire chocolate box contents had disappeared and the box appeared shredded and hanging awkwardly out of the fridge.

"What the heck?" she blurted out loud. Now she really did think the red wine had played a part in her hazy brain.

Could there possibly be a happy chocolate box reunion? The chocolates really didn't dare to hope. Could Tangerine Dreamer make it back to the box and how would she know where they were all hiding? It had been more than likely that she would be nibbled before then or simply discarded in the shiny kitchen rubbish bin with the remains of the dinner party and some mouldy French brie cheese. That would be the worst combination to be placed in a bin liner.

On the laundry room floor there lay a voluminous pair of crumpled jeans, that had made her escape so much easier thought Tangerine Dreamer as she squeezed herself out of the pocket. Had the others left her any clues, like the last time she had got separated from the group? The first clue had been the tiny paper chocolate description leaflet from their own chocolate box discarded on the floor in front of her. The second clue came once she had reached the kitchen and found a tiny smudge of melted caramel in a blob, on a shiny white floor tile. Not really obvious to the human eye, but if you lined this up it was directly in front of the long blue cupboard. Looking straight ahead there had been the final clue pointing her in the right direction. They made some tiny bunting flags out of miniature toothpicks and shreds of torn up kitchen roll then strung them on the chrome door handle. Working against the clock hoping that Tangerine Dreamer despite being a little squashed out of shape would make it back to their new home. But had all their clues been in vain? Would she have the strength to make her way back? Maybe she would be eaten at the last minute?

At two o'clock the kitchen lights went out again, the midnight feast completed. The chocolates settled down for a long but anxious night, unaware that their long time friend Tangerine Dreamer had been slowly making her way back to the chocolate team after her lucky escape. Quite a difficult feat, when you are misshapen, trying to find your way in the pitch darkness. The clues had been spot on and easy to follow. When daylight broke, there had been an excited chitter chatter amongst the remaining chocolates. Nestled, exhausted in the corner of the pile of baking sheets was their old friend. She had finally made it back in the early hours of the morning! Squeals of delight came from the shelf amid the obligatory chocolate hugs. What a celebration they had planned! It would be a truly joyous "Chocolate Box Reunion" for all concerned!

THE LITTLE RED DRESS

The tickets sold out weeks ago. The compere for the evening would be Edie McIntyre, a large personality built on a skinny frame. She was the Chief Executive of the local Arts Foundation and was really pleased she had attracted the right audience. Looking around the hotel ballroom Edie knew she had all the skills to make the charity fundraiser evening go with a comedic laugh and a bang. Rich and famous figures from the sporting, art and political worlds were expected at the Metropolitan Hotel. There might even be one or two politicians willing to put their hands in their pockets despite the deepening recession! Even the local MP Maurice Finch had agreed to show up, being in his home constituency it would be good form to show his face.

At two o'clock Secretary of State Maurice Finch stood up and asked his new secretary Tasha to order him a taxi for later that evening. Leaning round the doorframe

"Please can you cancel my appointments for this afternoon Tasha. I'm out of the office till tomorrow" The reminder popped up on his phone.

On the other side of town Maurice's eldest son Tommy had recently taken up art classes and was putting the final touches to his painting. Today, would be the last session. The students' ages ranged from Tommy at twenty-one to Vera at eighty-two. But his observational skills had greatly improved, as his hand moved more fluidly and instinctively over the canvas. The Arts Foundation sponsored the painting classes in the hope that a donation of some of the artwork would generate funds. The idea was that each week the tutor Mike Langton would pick out the best of the bunch. The French model Veronique showed up dressed in the tiniest of red cocktail dresses that spilled out at the top struggling to contain her voluminous bosoms. The zipper strained to breaking point had worked its way down her front so that her black lacy bra was fully exposed. Tommy struggled with his proportions. He urgently needed to learn how to replicate shape. Veronique was a true pro. Taking her place on the couch, she relaxed into the second hour of her pose. Suddenly Mike realised that he had forgotten his promise to get a portrait ready for the charity event that evening. Surveying the choices from today's session, most were sub-standard, but one had caught his eye. Eyeing the spidery signature on the bottom the lad had certainly depicted style and the form of the seductive dress and Veronique's ample charms. Edie McIntyre from the Arts Foundation sponsored the painting classes and was depending on him for a donation of a canvas.

Free from his office Maurice was out jogging through the park, under the beech trees that were already shedding their copper leaves. Returning hot and sweaty hot and sweaty from his run he headed straight to the shower. Emerging wrapped in a pink fluffy towel, he decided to lay his head on the goose-filled pillow telling himself five minutes shut-eye before heading out to the big event. An hour later he awoke, first, he noticed the light outside had changed from afternoon sunshine to early evening twilight. He flicked on the Murano glass light. Rubbing his eyes, focusing on the phone…Oh hell! Smoothing down his damp hair with some hair gel he yanked on his pants and trousers whilst tucking in his white dress shirt. Being lazy he had opted for the ready-to-wear red bow tie. Squeezing into his dinner jacket he checked his pockets for all the essentials. Tickets, phone, cash, and a hankie all seemed to be present and correct. The pre-ordered taxi arrived on time.

The painting class had finished on time, although the tutor seemed in a hurry to usher his students out of the door. Covering his chosen portrait in a large cloth and some bubble wrap he drove off towards the hotel. He had promised to deliver the top drawing of the week to the charity fundraising event. Selecting the best drawing of Veronique his top model which oddly enough belonged to the new lad in the group Tommy. He thought it depicted the style and form of the cocktail dress with a broken zip perfectly.

Maurice decided to head to the bar for a quick aperitif before kick-off. A Pastis with ice and water. He lounged against the pillar eyeing up the other bidders. The order of the evening was a four-course meal and then bidding for prizes would start as folks sipped on their coffee and liqueurs. The programme listing various prizes for donations was strategically placed next to each guest so one could decide in advance the item they wished to bid for. Maurice was seated next to the fliff fluff of Arts Society, some more affable than others, but not all his cup of tea.

Edie stood up and did her grand welcome and still Maurice had not so much as glanced at the programme. He always liked to wing it in these situations and see what came up. They breezed through the first six prizes of Weekends away for two, and expensive bottles of Burgundy. As Edie announced the seventh prize Maurice found himself face to face with a striking portrait of a woman in an unzipped red dress that looked awfully familiar. Maurice did a double-take. Suddenly feeling faint. Mopping his face with his handkerchief. On full view was the unmistakable form of Veronique wearing the red dress he had bought her the week before.

Too late the bidding had started. Who the hell had painted it? He decided to bid for it as Veronique would show her gratitude in her familiar exotic ways. "Three thousand pounds" he heard himself shout out. Edie smiled and turned to the crowd. "Congratulations goes to the most generous Right Honourable Maurice Finch MP for recognising the beauty of the sitter and the talent of his own son Tommy," said Edie with a knowing grin.

PINK GOGGLES

Mythical chameleons of the sea back in the nineteen sixties, the Mersalts lived at the bottom of a freshwater infinity pool in Malaysia, floating and swimming on the ever-changing tides. Aquatic time travellers, translucent in appearance, fluid in their movements, over millennia the creatures developed the power to transform themselves to obtain whatever they wanted. Cleverly avoiding the lurking sharks and rays that took such a keen interest in them. With firm tentacles they would gather objects in their vice like grip. They could hunt their prey whilst still forming, and never paused to sleep, always active. Renowned in the underwater world for getting their own way at any cost. They lived on the grace and favour of the tidal pools along the coastline, moving on to their next location when they had completed their mission and captured what they wanted.

Their eyes were a watery shade of pink, with long, sophisticated eyelashes, most unusual for an underwater creature. Seeing the world only through rose-coloured eyes, they were irresistibly drawn to all things coloured pink. No other creature found underwater was known to focus so specifically on the colour pink. Acting as independent entities with extrasensory cells, they used a force that quickly subdued their enemy. Thankfully for both humans and other mythical folk, they fed mainly on crabs and molluscs.

Lizzie was the second youngest of a family of seven, with bundles of dark curly hair that hung in ringlets around her chubby, freckled face. Her family had arrived from England on a three year naval posting to the Malaysian city of Johor Bahru. This would be Lizzie's home for the next three years. Where she would have the rich experience of living in a tropical climate. For the first time in her life she saw the branches of a palm tree floating and rustling on the warm humid breeze. Drawing these soon earned her the only good art marks she ever achieved, scoring her a proud ten out ten. For hours and hours she practiced in the garden at home with her sketch pad and coloured green pencils.

As well as new sights, there were new smells to get used to, some more pleasant than others, especially on market day.

Every afternoon since her family had arrived in Johor Bahru, Lizzie swam at the local freshwater tidal pool.(Schools in Malaysia only opened in the mornings.) The pool was lined with thousands of tiny square mosaic tiles. Crafted from turquoise porcelain, they were meticulously arranged in the style of the first tiles produced by the Greeks. A giant statue depicting a pod of leaping dolphins stood proudly at the pool's edge, spouting pink water to lure you into the depths of the pool and its mythical secrets (According to her parents Lizzie had always suffered with an overactive imagination). The children often perched on the backs of the dolphins, pretending to fly through the air, or swam under the water as it spouted forth from the dolphins 'mouths, Lizzie was adamant it had been pink last time she looked.

That day the only thing on Lizzie's mind was her missing pink goggles, her pride and joy.

"Mum, have you seen my pink goggles?" she shouted.

"Mark had better not have taken them down to the pool!" She had already ransacked Mark's bedroom. Now furious, she grabbed his rucksack and tipped its contents out across his bed. The very model of an irritating older brother, Mark was always borrowing her stuff. Little did Lizzie know how dangerous but important her infamous pink goggles would become in her next adventure.

"Found them," she shouted out. But as usual, no one was listening.

The goggles given to her for her eighth birthday by her dad, were extra special.

"These should help you improve your underwater swimming, Lizzie. Take good care of them won't you, and above all try not to lose them as they were very expensive" that was a warning. Lizzie noticed the label 'Speedo 'on the box. Lizzie had never had a pair of her own and she knew it would be imperative not to lose them. Everything her family owned was always for sharing. Despite writing her name in capitals in luminous green felt tip pen on all her possessions, Lizzie had fought a losing battle in keeping track of any of them.

The daily pool time was an entirely new experience as she made up new games, with her newly found school friends Louise, Kim, and Candy. The children all hung out together mainly at the bottom of the pool, where they each strove to become champion of the underwater 'holding your breath 'competition. This meant repeatedly diving down while proudly wearing an imaginary badge of honour. Beneath the surface of the water, their freedom was exhilarating. The strong saline liquid mixed with a dash of chlorine washed over them, giving them a warm embrace akin to a familiar hug. The girls were in a circle at the bottom of the pool holding their breath, waiting for the first one to give up and return to the surface. Lizzie was always one of the last to pop out of the water. Her eyes keen to see who was the winner.

During one of the daily swimming sessions the mythical Mersalt family decided to introduce themselves to Lizzie. They had spotted her weaving and gliding with rhythmic ease through the water. With their long tentacles and tendrils, they beckoned to her. The Mersalt family consisted of five members: a mother and father, with three children. The younger ones consisted of a small baby, an older sister, and a teenager. Though the teenager presented as a male, Lizzie was unsure what it was meant to be. Terror fought with curiosity in her mind as adrenaline rushed through her veins. None of her friends were visible as she glanced back over her shoulder. What? Suddenly she found herself unable to surface. Her focus blurred for a moment, making a blue haze of the swimming pool mosaics. There was an almighty force now holding her body back. Unsure exactly what she was looking at, Lizzie felt Mrs. Mersalt take her hand in a vice-like grip before leading her towards a mirror in the side of the pool. To Lizzie's astonishment they passed through the mirror and out the other side, crossing the line between mythology and actuality.

"But, what's happening?" thought Lizzie, her mind suddenly racing.

The Mersalts had considerable physical strength and the power to enable underwater breathing, which gave Lizzie a bizarre, unfamiliar sensation. Water no longer shot up her nose as it would normally do when you tried to breathe underwater. Lizzie wrinkled up her nose to try it out, but pulled a grimace when all she could taste was salt. There was no sense of urgency from her lungs to surface and breathe normally. It must have worked, as she was breathing underwater without assistance. Before she knew it she had descended into a watery underworld made entirely of pink. The flora and fauna were pink, with roots covered in pink candy floss. Lizzie grabbed some of the candy floss seaweed and tucked it into her swimsuit, thinking she might need it for later!

The furniture was pink, with a table and chairs arranged neatly around a circular pink rug. Food was laid out on the table, just like a buffet would be back at home. The Mersalts encouraged her to eat using just her fingers. She peeled the skin from pink avocados and pink bananas, and ate vibrant pink tomatoes whole. She washed the food down with a pink drink that tasted vaguely like a salty strawberry milkshake.

Mrs. Mersalt seemed particularly interested in the pink goggles, advancing towards them, admiring her reflection. Swimming closer to Lizzie's face, she stared intently at the pink plastic oval frames. Clearly, she wanted them for her little girl, to add to the family's collection of memorabilia. Hanging on the walls of their pink aquatic abode were flip flops, a bucket and spade, and a very squished hair scrunchy covered in pink fabric. These were just a few of the gems in their pink collection. Mother Mersalt was prepared to go to extreme lengths to obtain anything pink, as Lizzie was about to find out.

Lizzie had to think quickly, so played some underwater games with the young Mersalt children as a distraction: tug the tentacle, chase the flipper, and ring o' pink roses. The children were totally distracted but delighted, spending their time going round and round in circles. But wait… where had the mirror on the wall gone? That had been her escape route back! Lizzie had lost track of the direction that led her back to the pool. The sudden realisation was like a punch to her stomach. Determined not to cry, and with no help available, she decided to brave it out, and held back her salty tears in the pink watery underworld.

Suddenly Lizzie felt that she had awoken from another of her vivid dreams to discover this was reality. Until now she had been secretly enjoying her freedom, but it seemed there would be no leaving until Mrs. Mersalt had her tentacles on the chief prize: the pink goggles. For the moment Lizzie was effectively being held hostage beneath the water until she handed them over. Having been lured into a trap, she would need to quickly think of an escape plan before she got washed away into the pink kingdom for good. How on earth was she going to extricate herself?

Little did Lizzie know that the Mersalts had brought her across a time threshold and so nobody at home had even realised she was gone. How long did they plan to hold her hostage, as so far everything was communicated by sign language? There seemed a general reluctance to let her leave any time soon. Whenever she made her way towards the spot on the wall where she thought the glass mirror had been she was escorted firmly back. There was no door visible, nor any other way in and out of the pink kingdom. The only route had to be through the mirror on the side of the tank. But could she find the mirror that had disappeared the last time she looked? Lizzie was beginning to lose patience, so gave Mrs. Mersalt one of her infamous scowls. Unfortunately this did nothing whatsoever to further the escape plan. At that moment the stakes were too high.

Self-discipline was a large part of everyday life for Lizzie, who regularly practised swimming underwater to improve her stroke rate and to become the best at breath-holding techniques. Her competitive nature carried over into her swimming races. It had felt so good to finally be competent at something unrelated to schoolwork. The ability to hold her breath for an entire length of the pool without coming up for air was a significant accomplishment. This technique had already proven to be immensely helpful. The swimming gala had been the highlight of her stay in Johor Bahru to date. Winning all three of her races which resulted in a small cup and bar of chocolate for each success.

Lizzie's mind was preoccupied with fear of the consequences waiting for her when she eventually returned home, and the moment when she had to confess to her father that she had lost her expensive birthday goggles. He would not believe the story about pink creatures at the bottom of the swimming pool, demanding her goggles in exchange for her release! She would be in trouble, so she knew she would need to be economical with the truth. Lizzie's fear of returning home without the pink goggles was twofold. Firstly, it would result in a possible grounding, as she had been warned by her father; and secondly there would be no swimming, which would be really painful for her to bear. But if she was honest, her worst fear was that her family would have disappeared completely by the time she returned, having packed up the house again and left for England without her. How long had she been in the dayglo pink underworld so far? Was it a minute, an hour or a day? She had lost all sense of time. Who could say, perhaps she would become the first child time-traveller!

How would she explain the story of the Mersalts in the mythical underworld, taking her hostage under the water in exchange for her pink goggles? Who would believe that she had travelled through a magic mirror on the side of the swimming pool and eaten a meal consisting entirely of pink food? Her siblings would laugh out loud at the very idea. Luckily she had kept the pink candy floss as proof.

Lizzie accepted the time had come to exchange the goggles for her freedom. Release from the pink underworld was about to happen! Normally it would have been difficult to see under the water of the swimming pool without her goggles and her eyes would have been stinging, but down there she could see through the water perfectly.

More than anything else, her mind was made up by the thought of missing her dinner that night. She already knew what would be on the menu at home. Shepherd's pie followed by an apple crumble with custard, cream, or ice cream or simply all three together. This was all the incentive Lizzie needed. Reluctantly she peeled off the pink goggles, passing them over to the waiting Mrs. Mersalt (who had been holding out her tentacles expectantly). The little ones swam in excited circles, swishing their tendrils in ecstasy. It was hard to tell at what point Lizzie managed her escape and extricated herself back through the mirror. Everything still seemed very much the same as when she had left it an hour ago… but had it only been an hour? It was hard to tell.

Feeling a little dejected, Lizzie wandered home for her evening meal. Could life get much worse, really? She bit the inside of her mouth hard, determined to make it home on time. Strangely when she arrived, no one seemed to have missed her. Her brothers barely looked up from their comics as she walked into the kitchen. How strange it was as if she hadn't been away.

That evening at the table her father asked the dreaded question.

"How was your day, Lizzie?"

"Oh, the usual," she said calmly, looking at her plate, not wishing to catch his eye.

While they were clearing the dishes after dinner her father asked how she had come to lose the goggles. He knew! But, how? Lizzie thought carefully before answering, then confessed that the pink goggles had been lost at the bottom of the pool. A small white lie came into her head, perhaps someone had stolen them, but she thought better of it? The expression on her father's face told her she would be wise to tell him the truth. The frown was still there when she had finished explaining, but he really didn't seem too cross. His anger had all been in her imagination.

Each day Lizzie visited the poolside in the vain hope that her pink goggles would reappear, perhaps slung over a fence post or floating on the surface in the shallow end of the pool.

The seasons were on the turn. The tropical cyclones had ended and autumn cast long shadows ahead of its arrival. The summer tides were changing. The pink goggles had never been found, despite a long and desperate search by Lizzie and her friends. A small cloud of gloom had cast its shadow over the group. All her fondest memories were kept secretly below the water's surface.

What no one knew was that the pink goggles were on their way south, to another pink kingdom on the next tropical tidal flow. Baby Mersalt was wearing pink oval goggles especially for the journey, although they seemed a little large for such a small creature. All the pink objects had been gathered up and sent on ahead in a pink beach box by Mr. and Mrs. Mersalt, just like Lizzie's family had done with their own possessions not so long ago when they arrived in Johor Bahru. What the Mersalts had left behind by the pool was a discarded pair of blue swimming goggles. And was that a piece of pink avocado hiding under the sun lounger?

Walking back to her house after her daily search, Lizzie felt in the back pocket of her frayed denim shorts. Her fingers came across something saved from her visit to the mythical underworld: a piece of pink candy floss seaweed. Would it still taste the same above the waterline, in her own world? Unsure, but feeling brave, she tentatively nibbled the corner. She needn't have worried. It still tasted delicious, if a little salty! This cheered her up immensely.

About the Author

Fiona grew up in Hampshire, Dorset and Malaya before combining motherhood with a successful NHS career spanning twenty-five years. Her life experiences contribute significantly to the depth and substance of her writing. Her creative writing journey began with a gift of an entry fee for a story competition three years ago. Married for nearly forty years, she has two sons, two daughters-in-law and one delightful grandchild.

To date Fiona has written ten short stories, three are published in anthologies, and four are included in The Wedding Dress. One novel, Look Both Ways is currently in publication and due for release in late 2022. A semi-autobiography, Taking The Bandage, was released in 2021. The latest novel Inscription is due for release in 2023. Further information can be found on;
www.ballardsbookshelf.com

Printed in Great Britain
by Amazon

CHANGE HOW YOU USE YOUR MIND
MAKE PERSONAL SUCCESS A FACT
NOT A DREAM!

Achieve what you want in life:
- ▶ Using six mental laws for success.
- ▶ Harnessing the power of your subconscious mind.
- ▶ Boost your self-confidence and self-belief.

'The author explains in a psychological context how the mind works and how this knowledge can be used to improve the quality of your life in many positive ways.'

CHRIS SMITH
Former Director of WellMind Training Ltd

'This book does not indulge the reader with reasons why you cannot achieve what you want in life. Instead it suggests you become aware of what is stopping you.'

JENNY LYNN
Co Founder of the 'Open Mind College'

'Achieve What You Want In Life' includes the basic psychological concepts the author used during his 23 years as a successful professional therapist.

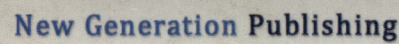

ISBN 978-1-910394-02-1

New Generation Publishing